D0186317

Dinosaurs go Christmas Shopping

TRICERATOPS
(tri-SERRA-tops)

STEGOSAURUS
(STEG-oh-SORE-us)

PTEROSAUR
(TERR-oh-sore)

HADROSAURUS
(HAD-row-SORE-us)

ANKYLOSAURUS
(an-KIE-loh-sore-us)

PARASAUROLOPHUS
(pa-ra-saw-ROL-off-us)

IGUANODON
(ig-WHA-noh-don)

SPINOSAURUS
(SPINE-oh-SORE-us)

TYRANNOSAURUS REX
(tie-RAN-oh-sore-us rex)

APATOSAURUS
(ah-PAT-oh-sore-us)

VELOCIRAPTOR
(vel-OSS-ee-rap-tor)

To Eoin and Ronan, with love
T.K.

For Mum, who taught me
how to put glitter on cards, the
earliest Christmas memory I have
S.W.

First published in 2018 by Scholastic Children's Books
Euston House, 24 Eversholt Street
London NW1 1DB
a division of Scholastic Ltd
www.scholastic.co.uk
London ~ New York ~ Toronto ~ Sydney ~ Auckland
Mexico City ~ New Delhi ~ Hong Kong

Dinosaurs go Christmas Shopping

Timothy Knapman ✳✳✳ Sarah Warburton

SCHOLASTIC

My Christmas is for presents,
And fun and Santa Claus,
I'd never want it spoiled
By naughty dinosaurs.

BAUBLES
for
SALE!

When Mum and I go shopping
To buy our Christmas tree
I look around for dinosaurs
And this is what I see...

Triceratops gets tangled up –
Trees topple as he falls!

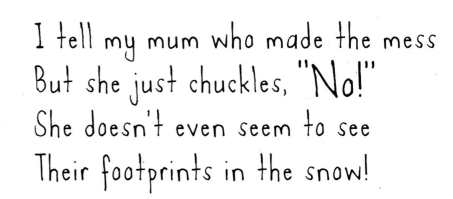

I tell my mum who made the mess
But she just chuckles, "No!"
She doesn't even seem to see
Their footprints in the snow!

And when we reach the shopping mall,
I watch them run and hide.
Why don't the grown-ups **notice** all
The dinosaurs inside?

Stegosaurus joins the choir
But – **ugh!** – he cannot sing,

While T-Rex in a Santa hat
Is gobbling everything!
Shes eaten up the Christmas pud,
The turkey, pies and cake...

And now she's munching Christmas cards!

She'll get a tummy ache!

Santa's
GROTTO
PLEASE WAIT HERE

I go and ask if Santa Claus
Will say, "Behave yourselves!"

But no – he's an apatosaur,
With Spinosaurus elves!

The pterosaurs steal stockings!

Iguanodon
breaks toys!

Can **anybody** save the day
For all us girls and boys?

"You Christmas shopping dinosaurs,
stop right now!" I shout.
"At Christmas time we must be kind –
that's what it's all about.

So please be good, and put things back
And clear this mess away.

It really would be **awful**
To ruin Christmas day."

Flop asks Pando to show everyone how to do
a **BIG** kick and a little kick.

"For a little kick, you do this," explains Pando.
He gently kicks the ball.

"So, for a little kick . . . you stand still and kick
the ball with the front of your foot," says Flop.

"I *like* doing little kicks," replies Sula.

"I want to do BIG kicks," says Bing.

"So do I!" says Pando.

"Ah, is this the *best* spot for a BIG kick, Pando?" Flop asks. "Is there anything *breakable* here?"

Sula points to the house. "Ohh, your windows, Flop."

"Indeed," says Flop.

Bing looks around the garden. "What about there?" He points to the back fence.

"For a **BIG** kick," says Pando, "you just . . . kick it!"

Pando runs forward and takes a big kick
and the ball flies forward.

BOOOFFF!

"Woohoo!" shouts Pando, celebrating.

"Good shot, Pando," says Flop. "So, for a BIG kick,
you take a run up before you swing your leg?"

"Yes," says Pando.

"Oh, oh! Can *I* have a go now?" asks Bing.

He steps back then *runs* up to the ball and . . .

his **foot** misses it.

Bing tries again. This time, he takes three steps back, then runs and kicks the ball towards the fence.

"Yay!" he cheers as it flies forward.

"Yay, Bing!" cheer Sula and Pando.

"*Well done*, Bing," says Flop.

Bing, Pando and Sula ask Flop if they can see who can
kick the ball the furthest.

"Can we use your planting pots,
please, Flop?" asks Bing.

"Sure," replies Flop. "I have orange, green or red."

Bing chooses orange, Sula chooses red and Pando chooses green.